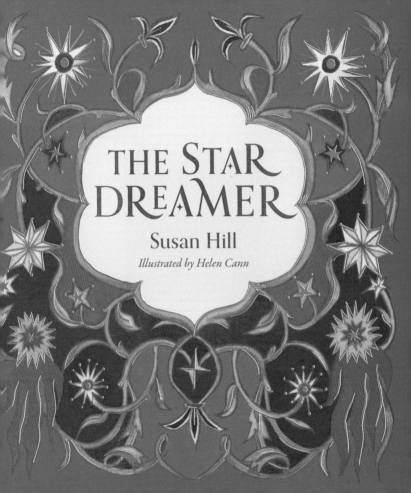

THE STAR
DREAMER

Susan Hill

Illustrated by Helen Cann

For Lila
S.H.

For Roger and Roxy
H.C.

PUBLISHED BY
LONG BARN BOOKS

Printed and bound in the EU on behalf of JFDi Print Services Ltd.

ISBN: 978-1-902421-16-2

LONG BARN BOOKS

'Wake up, boy! Wake up...' My father was shaking me and I was confused because it seemed that I had only just gone to sleep.

'Get dressed. Hurry.'

The lamps were not lit and the house was silent.

Outside, the night sky glittered with stars and silken moonlight shone across the sand.

My father was the baker in our village not far from the city, and we could see the lights of braziers and torches and the oil lamplight, that seemed to run up and down inside itself, like water. We heard the bells and the blowing of the ram's horn, the shouts of men as they shooed their animals through the narrow streets and called their wares in the market place.

I had gone there, slung on my father's back until I was old enough to ride the ass and later to walk proudly about. At five I was given a small basket of bread rolls to carry on my head and then I did not just walk, I strutted. On this momentous night, I was ten years old and what would be asked and expected of me should not have been asked of any child.

I had long dreamed my dreams, but not every night, and for the rest I slept soundly, woke and in between there was nothing. But sometimes I had the vivid and strange dreams and I told them to my father. They interested him so much he began to ask me every morning. 'Did you dream last night,

Aziz?' If I had, he would memorise my words.

I dreamed in letters, numbers, symbols, which I saw written in the sand and sometimes of monstrous animals, a donkey with a sheep's body, a camel with leathern wings. The background was always dark, set about with stars and planets. Comets would shoot across, trailing sparks, and the moon was huge and red, and in one dream, it turned to water.

My mother told me that I could keep my dreams to myself if I preferred.

'They are yours, Aziz. Your father tells others because he is proud of a son who dreams such dreams. He says they are important.'

   9

I laughed at this but she did not and after that I often wondered who else had been told my dreams, and why.

'Keep close to me. Keep up.'

'Where are we going?'

No answer.

When we reached the city we went in the shadow of the wall. 'I wish we could go back home.'

No answer.

After a few minutes, we saw the lights of an encampment, surrounded by flares to keep the wild animals away. There were three large tents, with openings that gave a glimpse inside of red and gold rugs laid on the ground and draped over mounds of sand for seating. The lamp oils were coloured ruby and topaz. Strings of brass bells hung in the doorways, and animal harnesses on stakes outside. I heard the camels tossing their heads and stamping the ground softly, and men's voices.

A sentry gestured us to follow and then we were stepping out of the cold night into a tent, and from starlit black into glowing colours and coals burning in a brazier. A man in grey robes sat beside a leathern stool, on which were several open books, a turban wound like a fat snake round his head.

He looked at me steadily and I saw great wisdom in his eyes, and kindness.

'The boy who dreams dreams,' he said.

'Yes.' But then I added, 'Sometimes,' because he looked like a man who would require the truth.

'Why am I here and when can I go home?' It was my father I asked but then I realised that he was no longer there and I felt fear clench a fist inside me.

'You are coming on a journey. We need you because your dreams may guide us.'

'Who are you? Where will we go? When...'

He raised his hand. 'You will go to your tent and sleep and if you dream you must come and tell me at once.'

The servant led me to a smaller tent, dark and without hangings and rugs, but close to a brazier. I had a mat, a blanket, and a folded sack for my pillow.

'Sleep.'

I was shivering too much and too numb to cry, let alone rest. I heard the snorting and head-tossing of the camels. After a long time, I did sleep.

'Did you dream?'

He was standing over me.

I shook my head, too afraid to speak.

'Eat now. And dream tonight.'

Outside, dawn had broken, the sun was a great copper gong and I was given a place among the attendants to feed. They were kind enough but looked at me curiously, as if I were a strange beast. I was troubled and remained silent but I learned things from their talk. Besides Balthasar, there were two others, great scholars of astronomy, seers of the future, and all of them had been excited by the appearance of a new and brilliant star in the eastern sky. Our journey was somehow connected with that star but nobody seemed to know any more and I heard nothing else until I was taken before Balthasar again. I went, praying that I would be sent home because I had not dreamed.

Balthasar was sitting before a chart.

'Come here. Do you know what these are, Aziz?'

I stared hard at the scroll. 'Stars in the night sky.'

'Have you ever dreamed of the stars?'

'Yes.'

'Do you know who is the king?'

 17

'Herod. He is a great king, my father told me, but I have never seen him.'

Balthasar touched one of his books. 'In here is told how a far greater king than Herod will be born and the way to his birthplace will be shown by a brilliant new star. The great wonder is that we have seen it, after searching the skies for years, and now we must follow where it leads us. When we find the place, we have orders to direct King Herod there, so that he may go and worship the new young king.'

I thought about this for some minutes before I asked, 'What has this to do with my dreams?'

'It will be hard to follow just one star out of the whole night sky but if we fail King Herod...'

There was a silence and a great chill touched my heart.

'But our way may be shown us in one of your dreams.'

The chill deepened and I was very afraid. I could not dream to anyone's order.

I saw in Balthasar's eyes that he was troubled and did not want to fail him. There were only two things I could do – sleep and, before I slept, pray as best I knew.

I felt as if I had grown up suddenly and come to understand things I had not been taught. I felt responsible, no longer a child walking in men's footsteps, and I sensed that the wise man knew this.

He stood and beckoned but I hung back, afraid I would let him down. Balthasar put his hands on my shoulders. 'You will not fail. You are the boy who dreams.'

Before I slept I knelt and prayed, not in words I had learned from my father but in my own. Then I slept soundly, but though I did not dream on that night or for the next four, Balthasar remained patient.

On the fifth morning I woke not from dreams, but hearing a voice that seemed to speak inside my head, and certain in my heart that I must do as it told me.

'When night falls and the star rises in the east, we start,' I told Balthasar. 'You must go first, I will ride beside you and the voice will guide me, following the star correctly.'

All day the camp was astir, and everything was being packed up, animals, tents and equipment, food and great leathern bags of water. At sunset, the three sages, Balthasar, Caspar and Melchior, mounted their camels and I was given an old, steady ass to ride. Part of me was afraid and choked with longing for home, but I was excited too, and grave with responsibility.

The star was brilliant in the eastern sky at night and even visible by day, and we followed it easily and made steady progress. But then the days began to shorten and the track became steep and rough; the nights were bitter, with an icy wind blowing sand and dirt and, later, frozen snow in our eyes. The camels became unsteady on their feet and even my strong little ass stumbled and swayed as we climbed. The rocks were bare so that we could not pitch any sheltering tents and everyone huddled closely together with only the breath of the beasts for warmth. I shivered, my skin felt raw and when I lay down, the rocky ground cut into my flesh and bruised my bones.

  24

The servants began to murmur against me, saying that I was leading them the wrong way, and when we came higher still, into deep snow and ice, even Balthasar questioned me. But the voice in my head was clear, the star was brilliant ahead. It grew so cold that we could not lie down for fear we would freeze to death, and then I lost my confidence and became more afraid. I no longer cared about seeing the new king.

But after many more terrible days and nights, we began to descend, the track became easier, and we left snow behind, though it was still bitterly cold. Once or twice I saw fires in distant fields,

where the shepherds guarded their sheep, and at last, at last, lights from buildings.

The star no longer went ahead but stopped, low in the sky.

I heard singing, sweet, sweet voices and then I began to cry, out of exhaustion and homesickness, and also relief and joy.

The star stood over a stable behind an inn. The servants and animals crowded outside – only the three wise men were to go in but then Balthasar pushed me forward, and so I went too. The light inside the stone stable was dim and yet somehow it was the brightest light I had ever seen. What we saw was so ordinary and humble yet astonishing, a

mother, a father, a baby, with so many visitors
and animals, that the small stable was crowded.
I looked down at the boy, quietly sleeping, and he
was indeed just a baby, and looked the same as all
the other babies I had seen in my own village, and
yet I knew at once that he was not.

We had come so far, on the worst of journeys,
but we stayed only a short time and then we were
out in the darkness again and I was dazed and all
the energy and excitement drained out of me.

We camped just outside Bethlehem and I knew
from what I had overheard on the way that now
we had found the new king, the message must
go at once to King Herod, so that he too could

come to worship him. I felt very different, as if a grey shroud wrapped me round and a heavy weight pressed down upon me. The thought of our return over the icy windswept mountain darkened my mind.

I huddled into my blanket and slept, and at once I began to dream terrifyingly, of blood and swords and fighting men, and children crying in fear and a starless night sky.

I woke and tried to sit up but my eyes closed and I fell and down, down again, into the swirling pit of flashing swords, dying babies and women crying, wolves howling, and billows of smoke and flames in the sky.

At dawn I went to Balthasar, and he sent the servant to bring me a scalding, bitter drink, which he made me

sip before he would let me speak. It seemed to set fire
to my throat and then my belly, but after only a few
seconds, I felt recovered enough to tell my dreams.

'What does all this mean? Have you ever known
such dreadful images?'

I had not, but that night I dreamed them again, and
after that an invisible finger drew a map in the sand,
pausing every so often so that I could memorise it. A
brilliant light shone upon me, not a light to see by but a
light of understanding.

'There is great danger. We must go home another
way.' And I copied the map on the ground.

'That route will take us many weeks. Why would we
take it?'

'Because King Herod is furiously angry and jealous and must not find us. He will have his soldiers kill us because we have visited the new king and worshipped him.'

'No, no, Aziz, Herod is a good man, a great king. Your dream is wrong.'

'My dreams do not lie. I know this, I know it to be true.'

After being silent and thoughtful for a long time, Balthasar said: 'We will leave tonight and travel your way.'

The journey across endless desert and plains was long and tiring, our food ran short and we had to ration it for the animals, and worst of all, feared we would run out of water. The men were footsore and weary and longed

for home, and on some days even the camels lay
down and refused to move for hours, but the miracle
was that we did not face any grave dangers, not even
from ravenous wild beasts, which always threatened
travellers, nor did we starve, and several times we came
upon unexpected oases from which we could drink
and draw water to store in the flagons. We met no one,
heard no news, but every day brought us nearer home
and when we saw the first shimmering line of the city
far ahead, there were great shouts of joy.

* * *

How could I have known the end of the story? That my father came running, the moment news came, took me roughly in his arms at once and then made me run with him; that my mother stood in the doorway and, as she saw me, burst into tears. 'See how you have grown, you are taller and stronger!'

I laughed and laughed and tried to wipe away her tears. I said: 'Ah, I am not your baby boy now.'

'Don't worry about that. Come and see.'

I saw. A wooden crib. Our old dog lying guard at its foot.

'Now I have a tall, strong young man,' my mother said, weeping all over again, 'and a baby boy.'

I stared in wonder at the baby in the crib. At my brother.

'The greatest miracle of all,' my father said, beside me, 'is that he escaped the sword. King Herod's soldiers came looking for every boy child under the age of two, and the stories are terrible, of how they snatched them away and slaughtered them. But news travelled ahead, as news does, and some were hidden safely. Some. Not all.'

'How did you hide him? Where did you go?'

'There was no need, he was not born until the day after the soldiers left.'

I bent down then and picked up my new brother and held him in my arms and he lay there quietly, looking up at me, and I felt a great love, as I had felt for the other baby, and with the same wonder and awe, and I said a silent prayer of thanks that they had both escaped the sword.

Though inside my head, the quiet voice spoke to me again, saying 'This time. But do not look ahead, Aziz. Do not look.'